THE
ACCIDENTAL
WITCH

ANNE MAZER

Hyperion Books for Children
New York

To my grandmother, Jean Fox,
a great reader, writer, and a killer Scrabble player
—A. M.

Text © 1995 by Anne Mazer.

FIRST EDITION
1 3 5 7 9 10 8 6 4 2

Library of Congress Cataloging-in-Publication Data
Mazer, Anne.
The accidental witch / Anne Mazer — 1st ed.
p.   cm.
Summary: Ten-year-old Phoebe is thrilled when she accidentally becomes a novice witch but soon wonders if she will ever develop and control her powers.
ISBN 0-7868-0088-7 (trade) — ISBN 0-7868-2073-X (lib. bdg.)
[1. Witches—Fiction. 2. Magic—Fiction.] I. Title.
PZ7.M47396Ac 1995
[Fic]—dc20   94-44284

This book is set in 13-point Hiroshige Book.

Designed by Lara S. Demberg.

CONTENTS

BEE FOR 1 SHORT

I've wanted to be a witch since I was four years old.

That was when the witches transformed a rusty, dried-up old park near our house into an oasis for parents and kids.

One night I saw the witches roosting on the withered trees. In the morning the trees were all in bloom, and in the park there were swings and slides, a fountain, beds of flowers, and a carousel that looked like a circus, a parade, and a wedding cake all at once.

Since then I've always dreamed of being a witch.

To tell the truth, I'm not exactly witch material.

I never go near a broom—or even a vacuum cleaner.

And cats make my eyes puff up.

My hair isn't long and black and flowing, either. It's short and straw colored and sticks up where it should curl or lie flat.

I once won a spelling bee, but I don't know anything about spells. Speaking of bees, my name is Phoebe, but I'm called Bee for short. I look something like a bee, except that I never wear yellow. Or black for that matter. Now if I were a witch, I might wear it a little more often.

It was International Spotlight on Witches Week in our class. We roasted our lunches over a bonfire, adopted a stray black cat, and put on a play about the old dark times when witches were banned.

Mr. Belkey, our fifth-grade teacher, said, "Without the witches, we'd all dry up like a box of raisins."

It had to be true. The witches possessed a special power that kept our world going. Witches put the colors in rainbows, the shine in a cat's fur, the reflection in mirrors.

Now we were studying witch lore. On the blackboard, Mr. Belkey had a list of superstitions and sayings about witches:

2

Witches and wishes go together.
A witch at night means luck in the light.
Stamp on a crack; save a witch's back.

"Which of these sayings are true and which are false?" Mr. Belkey asked. He was plump and pink, and round like an egg.

I flung my hand up and caught Peter Cook on the nose. "Sorry," I muttered. Peter was so thin and slight he was almost invisible, but somehow I always managed to knock into him.

"All true, Mr. Belkey!" Mandy said, glancing at the Apples. They gazed back at her adoringly.

Mandy looked like an ice-cream cone with sprinkles. She was leader of the Apples and she was *not* sweet.

"I admire your enthusiasm for the witches, Mandy," said Mr. Belkey. "But we must introduce the scientific method." He wiped a dimpled hand across his face. "Class, I want you to test out the ancient sayings. Find out if you stamp on a crack, will you *really* save a witch's back?"

"Of course," Mandy said.

"Superstitions such as these have always been taken for granted," Mr. Belkey said. "Now you have a chance to prove whether they are true or false. Perhaps one of you will make witch history."

"*I* will, Mr. Belkey!" Mandy said.

"Is she for real?" I asked Jennifer.

Jennifer shrugged. Lately, she was always hanging around the Apples, Mandy's band of adoring followers, even though she had been my best friend since preschool. We had shared witch games for years. We used to love to play at witches. We'd wave our hands and pretend to make the sun come out. Or jump off fences, pretending to fly.

Once, I danced around a tree and chanted some made-up words. Suddenly it began to rain.

"I made it rain!" I said.

The rain fell harder and harder. I opened my arms to gather it in. So this was what it felt like to be a witch! After that, even though I never got it to rain again, I wanted to be a witch more than ever.

"What are you going to do for your witch experiment?" I asked Jennifer on the way home.

"I don't know yet," she said.

I knew what I was going to do. I had known right away.

It was something I had read in *A Child's Garden of Witches*. "Witch in the mirror, witch and a moon. If you catch them both, you'll catch a

4

boon!" All I had to do was line up a witch and the moon in a mirror, and I'd catch witches' powers for twenty-four hours.

If I caught powers on Sunday night, I could fly into class on Monday and cast a spell or two before math.

Jennifer would be so thrilled. She would be proud to call me her friend. Maybe she would even forget about Mandy and the Apples.

As for Mandy and her Apples, they would turn green. And Mr. Belkey would have to give me an A+.

WITCHES' POWERS FOR TWENTY-FOUR HOURS

I sat in front of my open bedroom window with a pocket mirror in my hand and chanted, "Powers, powers, powers for twenty-four hours . . ."

It was cool outside, and the moon was full. I was so lucky! According to the book, this was the best time of the month to catch witches' powers.

Faraway in the darkening skies, I saw half a dozen witches flying toward our town.

The witches appeared small, smaller than the witch dolls that lined my room. Just like my dolls, they wore peaked hats and long capes, which billowed out behind them.

I tightened my grip on the mirror and tilted it so the

full moon was reflected directly in its center.

Now all I needed was a witch to fly across the moon.

Of course, even then I might not gain any powers. No one I knew had ever done it. And, anyway, it might just be another old witches' tale, like "To reach a witch, roll in mud."

I hoped Mandy would pick *that* one to test out.

I hoped *my* superstition would turn out to be the true one.

The witches were coming closer. I heard a low hum. It grew to a whir and filled the sky.

Capes crackled with wind, brooms swept away clouds.

The lead witch was riding straight for the moon. Her long gray hair streamed in the wind.

I was going to do it! "Yippee!" I yelled. I jumped from my seat and lunged closer to the window.

Then it happened. I stumbled over my feet and dropped the mirror.

The witch flew past the moon.

The mirror shivered, sighed, and broke into a thousand pieces.

*   *   *

When my mother came into my room to say good night to me, I was sweeping. Tiny slivers of glass were scattered everywhere—over the floor, under the bed, even in the closet.

"What broke, Bee?"

"Just a mirror."

My mother sighed. "Not the one I gave you for your birthday!"

"Sorry, Mom. It was an accident."

"It always is," she agreed.

Disasters follow me. I can't brush my teeth without spraying toothpaste over my clothes. I can't pop popcorn without it flying all over the kitchen. I can't even hand my mom a glass of water without spilling it in her lap. I'm the last one chosen for volleyball because I always drop the ball.

And the hamster always escapes when it's my turn to clean his cage.

Maybe someday I'll be like my mother. Buttons never fall off her clothes. Dishes don't drop from her hands. She was even a tennis champion in high school. If I can pick up a racquet without breaking something with it, I count it a good day.

"What were you doing with the mirror, Bee?" my mother asked. "Though I'm not sure I want to know."

"My homework assignment." I swept glass into the dustpan. "I was trying to catch witches' powers in the mirror. And I almost caught them, Mom!"

My mother looked worried. "Bee, trying to catch witches' powers is serious stuff. You could get hurt."

"Mom, someday I want to be a witch."

"You, Bee?" My mother shook her head. "Gaining witches' powers is not easy. You have to go through a long, arduous training. And the witches guard their magic carefully."

"But I *really* want to be a witch."

"If just anyone could have magic—then it wouldn't be magic, would it? Anyway, Bee, I don't think you could handle it."

"I could, Mom! I'm sure I could."

"You don't know anything about it, Bee. You're too young. Too starry-eyed. You don't see the reality of what it means to be a witch."

"I know, I know," I said. I leaned on the broom. Maybe she was right, but I couldn't help dreaming. I could just see myself flying over trees, casting spells, making flowers bloom in the gravel of the school-yard. And maybe turning Mandy into a plastic apple and giving her to Mr. Belkey on Teachers' Day.

"Bee . . . Bee . . ." My mother waved her hands in front of my face. "Earth to Bee!"

"Yes, Mom?"

"You remind me of your father, Bee. Head in the clouds, feet two inches above the ground. He never saw what was in front of his nose."

We were both silent for a moment. My father died when I was little; I really don't remember him at all.

"Maybe being a witch would help me be more practical, Mom. Think about it. What if the mirror had worked? It *almost* did."

"I'd rather not think about it. You, with witches' powers? Haven't you learned yet, Bee? You have to walk before you can fly."

My mom gave me one of those long, steady gazes—the kind that made me feel about two years old. "Maybe someday, Bee." She hugged me. "In ten years or so. It's a question of maturity, of dedication, of coordination."

"Yes, Mom." Was that all? Dedication I knew I had. Maturity would come someday, maybe a lot sooner than my mother thought. Coordination was the only thing I really lacked, and I could work on that.

EXPERIMENT ACCIDENT

Who will be first to present the results of their experiment?" Mr. Belkey asked on Monday.

"Me, Mr. Belkey!" Mandy said. She pranced to the head of the class and clasped her hands in front of her.

"What superstition did you pick, Mandy?"

"If you see a witch on the end of your bed, your wishes will come true," Mandy recited.

The Apples oohed.

"Did you see one?" Mr. Belkey asked.

Mandy smiled one of her sickening smiles. "Of course I did, Mr. Belkey. I see witches on the end of my bed all the time. My wishes *always* come true."

The Apples aahed.

"Yeah, right . . . ," I muttered to Jennifer.

"So you believe this superstition is true," Mr. Belkey said.

"Absolutely," Mandy answered.

"An example, please."

"My wish this week," she announced, "is to be the best student in the school in every way."

The Apples applauded.

Mr. Belkey beamed. "Very good, Mandy. I can tell you are almost there already."

"Of course," Mandy said. "And the witches will make sure I stay there." She flounced back to her seat.

"Anyone else?" Mr. Belkey asked. "Jennifer?"

Jennifer stood up at her desk. "'Witches' brew is good for you.' I drank a whole cup this weekend. The ingredients were one can of soda, one jar of peanut butter, a dribble of vanilla fudge, two rotten bananas, dill, parsley, and pepper."

"And? You had a stomachache?"

"No, my older brother and I raced across the park and I won."

"You attribute this to the witches' brew?" Mr. Belkey said.

"I've never beaten him before."

The class murmured in approval. Jennifer sat down. I raised my hand.

"Phoebe? Tell us about your experiment."

"I had a mirror. The witches were flying toward the moon. I only had to catch the witch and the moon in my mirror at the same time to gain witches' powers!"

"My goodness! And did you gain these powers?"

"Her?" Mandy sneered. "The only powers she could gain are pip-squeak powers."

"I had the moon in the mirror!" I said. "I had a corner of the witch's skirt in the mirror, too!"

Peter Cook stared at me.

"Yes, Phoebe? And then?" Mr. Belkey said.

"Well . . . then I stumbled."

"Oh, Phoebe," Jennifer sighed.

"And I dropped the mirror, and it broke."

Mandy and the Apples snickered.

"A little accident," I said. "It could have happened to anyone."

Though it probably wouldn't have.

Mr. Belkey clapped his hands. "I have a surprise for you, class. Tomorrow, a real witch is going to visit us."

"Hooray!" I said.

"Her name is Andelica. She is senior witch of the Fifth Sector, and she'll be here at exactly two minutes past two. I've done a little research, and I found out that a witch's favorite midafternoon snack is scones and tea."

"How wonderful of you, Mr. Belkey!" Mandy said.

Mr. Belkey beamed. "Senior Witch Andelica will tell us what the witches really do and exactly what kind of people they look for as apprentices."

Mandy pointed to herself. The Apples gazed reverently at her. "She'll love you," one of them said.

She might not love me—especially if Mandy was there hogging all the attention.

It was rumored that a senior witch could spot talent instantly, and if she saw the gift, even in a ten year old, she would take her and train her as an apprentice witch.

I hoped it was true and not another superstition.

I hoped she would spot the gift in me.

If I were a witch, I'd be less clumsy. My mother would have more confidence in me.

Jennifer would stay my friend. And Mandy and her Apples wouldn't pick on me all the time.

I *had* to get Senior Witch Andelica to notice me.

THE
BEAUTIFUL WITCH

On the day of Andelica's visit to our class everyone was guessing what she would look like.

"Twisted and ugly," one of the Apples said. "Only the junior witches are pretty."

"Mandy could be a junior witch," another Apple said.

"How many warts do you think she has?" Peter Cook asked.

"Do you think she'll change us into frogs or toads?" Jennifer asked.

"Don't be stupid," Mandy said.

Jennifer's face fell.

At 2:10, Mr. Belkey said, "I don't know what's

keeping this witch. So unreliable. I'll give her ten more minutes, then we'll have to go back to our regular work."

I groaned loudly.

I *had* to meet Andelica.

The venetian blinds on the windows clattered, and a strong breeze gusted through the room.

There was a puff of smoke and a faint burning smell.

Andelica, senior witch of the Fifth Sector, stood before us.

Senior Witch Andelica was young—and beautiful. Her long black hair hung almost to her waist; her skin was pale, her eyes gray and piercing. She wore an oversize purple-and-black sweater, black leggings, and acid purple socks.

A gray cat with a hot pink collar perched on her shoulder.

Her broom was long and sleek, with neon colors swirling through it. Andelica rested one slender hand on the broom and darted fierce glances at the class.

Mr. Belkey turned pale as an egg and edged toward the door. No one said a word.

"We fly through the skies, cast enchantments, and are part of the great sisterhood of witches," Andelica sang out.

"We weave spells for matters great and small. We weave stories as well—stories for the rain, snow, and wind, and stories for men and women, girls and boys."

I tried to get closer, but Mandy stuck out her elbows. "Buzz off, Bumble Bee," she hissed.

I stepped back—onto Peter Cook's foot.

"Oww, Phoebe!" he said.

"Sorry, Peter," I whispered.

"Most witches come to us at fourteen," Andelica continued, "though we take on very few as young as ten or eleven, if the time is right and they have the gift."

I looked over at Jennifer and pointed to myself.

"We use light powers lightly. We use strong powers secretly. We never use our powers carelessly.

"The colors of rain, dusty winds, and gutters of muddy water may all carry magic into your world."

I imagined secret rivers of magic seeping into the world, and I wanted to be a witch more than ever.

Peter Cook raised his hand. "How do you become a witch?"

Andelica pulled out a sheaf of orange papers and passed them out. She handed each of us a black pencil embossed with gray cats.

"Who among you dreams about joining the witches of Sector Five?"

My hand shot up. So did Mandy's hand and all the Apples' hands, like a wavy fence that hid me from view. How was Andelica ever going to notice me?

"There are many, many stages to becoming a witch," Andelica said. "Today I'll tell you about the main ones.

"The Four Stages to Witchhood," Andelica announced. "Stage one, readiness. Do you really want to be a witch? Do you long for it? Do you think about it all the time? Answer on the first line."

"YES," I wrote with my black pencil.

"Preparation is the next stage. You begin to learn about the witches. We witches have our own world and rules and activities."

Andelica stroked the gray cat. "Many of the rules you are not privileged to learn until you are actually a witch."

"I'm ready!" I wrote.

"The third stage is initiation." Andelica continued. "The aspiring witch must pass many tests to prove her readiness and to see if she has the strength and talent to become a witch."

"I do! Yes!" I put under stage three.

"In the fourth stage she is accepted as a novice to

be tested, trained, and observed, until she is ready to assume the mantle of full witchhood."

"Yes again!" I wrote. "Yes, yes, yes, I agree to everything."

And again I saw myself in black with a swirling cape, swooping into the sky on a fast-moving broom, a tall black hat on my head, doing wild and wonderful deeds.

Peter raised his hand again. "Can boys become witches?"

"Almost never," Andelica said. "Most boys can train as warlocks, who are our companions. However, their powers are not as great as ours."

Peter looked disappointed.

The piercing gray eyes of the witch took in every girl in the class.

"Who among you will have the perseverance, the discipline, the strength of will to train for long years as an apprentice witch?"

"Me!" Mandy had on her best apple-polishing expression and was gazing soulfully at Andelica. "Right over here! Me, Your Witchness!"

I tried to move toward Andelica again, but I couldn't get through the knot of Apples in front of me.

Mandy was waving her hand practically in Andelica's face. "Me, Your Greatness. Me, *me!*"

How could I ever get Andelica's attention?

"Make way, make way. Hot tea coming through. Or should I say witches' brew. Heh, heh, heh." Mr. Belkey, pink and plump, was carrying a large tray crowded with jam and scones and tea in flowered cups.

I saw my chance. "I'll take that, Mr. Belkey."

"Why, how courteous of you, Phoebe."

I grabbed the tray by its handles. Saucers clattered, scones jiggled, tea sloshed.

The kids around me all jumped away.

"Is he crazy letting her carry that?" one of the Apples said.

"I can't believe this," Mandy said. "Watch Fumble Bee lose it."

I finally reached the front of the room and stood in front of Andelica.

"I love tea," said the beautiful witch, smiling fiercely at me.

I smiled back at her—not so fiercely. "I love witches—," I began.

Someone shoved me.

The tray leaped. Teapot, teacups, spoons, saucers, scones, jam, cream, and sugar jiggled. Tea splattered over me—and Andelica, soaking her oversize purple-and-black sweater, her black leggings, and even her acid purple socks.

"Clumsy!" Andelica hissed, wiping a glob of raspberry jam from her face.

Jennifer groaned.

The Apples moaned.

Peter Cook covered his eyes.

"Change Phoebe into a toad!" Mandy yelled.

I grabbcd a napkin and started wiping jam from Andelica's cape.

The gray cat with the pink collar jumped onto the windowsill and screeched.

Mr. Belkey was on his hands and knees picking up broken pieces of teacup and sweeping up little piles of sugar.

"Stand aside!" Andelica snapped her fingers. *"Tea and scones. Jam and pot. Sugar, cream. Lift this blot!"*

Her clothes dried out, the cups flew together and onto the tray, the scones piled themselves neatly on a plate, tea sloshed back into the cups, and Mr. Belkey jumped up, looking like a bright pink Easter egg.

I was left holding a clean napkin.

But my clothes were still covered with tea and jam. Andelica had left me out of her magic snap.

MY MAGIC SNAP

5

When I got home, I decided to surprise my mother. The kitchen floor was sticky and dirty. So was I. At least one of us could get clean. I filled the pail with water and detergent.

Then the phone rang. It was Jennifer. "How did you ever get the nerve to bring that tea to Andelica!" she asked.

"I wanted to get close."

"That's so brave of you, Bee. What if she had changed you into a snake or a toad? You're lucky you're still a person."

"Yeah."

"You must have known you were going to spill it."

"Thanks to Mandy," I looked down at my tea-and jam-stained clothes. "She pushed me."

"Oh come on, Bee! Everyone knows you trip over your own shadow."

"Whose friend are you, anyway?" I asked.

"Mandy's not so bad," Jennifer said. "She's nice to me."

There was a short silence.

"I'm through with witches after today," said Jennifer. "I'm going to be an accountant when I grow up."

"But, Jennifer . . ." I felt so disappointed. "That's *boring*! Don't you want to cast spells? Don't you want to meet a warlock? Don't you want to fly at least once in your life?"

"No, Bee, I do not."

"Why not?"

"I'm scared of heights, and besides, there's no job security," Jennifer said. "No paid vacations, no health insurance. And that Andelica would be a tough boss."

She was probably right about that, I thought, as I hung up the phone. But, if anything, I now admired the witches even more. Andelica's power, her grace, her beauty. Her snap of the fingers—wouldn't that be handy!

I snapped my fingers over the uncleared table, then over the floor. "Rice Krispies, tablecloth, sugar bowl!" I sang out, trying to sound like Andelica. "Dust balls, wet mop, garbage can!"

Nothing happened.

I waved my arms. Still nothing.

I got out the broom and pretended I was soaring over the city.

If I were a witch, I'd be tall and slender and beautiful, with long pink-and-purple fingernails.

If I were a witch I'd never worry about Jennifer liking Mandy better than me. And Mandy would be too afraid of me to ever bother me again. My witches' powers would take care of everything.

My mother arrived home just as I was sailing through the sky. I was scattering tiny heart-shaped candies to the crowd of children below, and they were waving to me.

My mother backed in through the kitchen door, her arms full of packages, and tripped over the pail of water.

"Awww, Ma," I said.

"Ooh, Bee," my mother said.

We both stared at the pool of water on the floor.

"I was getting ready to mop," I said.

"On a broom?"

My mother has known me a long time, but she still isn't used to me.

She picked her way over the wet floor. Her shoes squished.

"Don't worry, Mom, I'll have the floor mopped and

dried in no time."

I snapped my fingers, but the floor stayed wet and slippery.

I snapped my fingers again. It was worth another try.

Then I got the mop to do it the old-fashioned way.

INTO THE CIRCLE

I was sitting in my favorite tree in the cemetery. Whenever I needed to think, I climbed the tree and hid in its branches. It was in a part of the cemetery that people rarely visited. The gravestones were old and tilted, the grass long and fragrant.

I thought about Jennifer and how she and I didn't seem interested in the same things anymore.

I thought of Mandy and how she had picked on me even more since she and Jennifer started becoming friends.

And I thought of Andelica and how I had spilled tea on her. I had probably ruined my chances forever of becoming a witch.

Speaking of Andelica, there she was.

I blinked and rubbed my eyes.

She *was* really there. She hadn't been under the tree a moment before, but she was standing there now.

Her eyes were closed. She was wearing a dark shiny skirt with pink lace at the edges and a necklace of oddly shaped stones. Her lips moved slightly, and the beads on her necklace glowed and flashed.

She began to pace a worn patch of grass, placing her feet precisely, as though she were following an invisible pattern. What was she doing? Casting a spell? Weaving a magical story that would come true? Fixing up the weather? It had been awfully cloudy lately.

I remembered Andelica had told our class that witches couldn't always let the sun shine. There was a balance they had to maintain.

Wouldn't it be great if she was casting a spell to make Mandy nicer to me?

I lay along the branch as still as I could and watched.

The wind fluttered the leaves on the tree and puffed out Andelica's shiny black skirt.

She began to move faster, to turn, to chant. "Stars, bars, witches and riches, brooms and dooms, hair and rare . . ."

My breathing quickened. I felt caught in her enchantment, as though a sticky net had been thrown over me.

"Insects, mice, and sickening spice . . ."

The air chilled and darkened, as though someone had clapped an iron bowl over the earth. The wind rose, and clouds sailed over the treetops.

Andelica moved faster and faster, spinning around the worn patch of grass. "Yellow toads and sticky roads . . . send them all to me!"

Leaves scudded. Birds disappeared. I clung to the branch.

"The broom flies up, the broom flies down . . . witches, witches in the town!"

The words clanged and crashed like metal pots.

The clouds had merged into a towering black wall. The darkness parted, and something even darker emerged, a long streaking mass, like a ragged dark flag hung from a pirate ship.

Swooping and swirling, shrieking and diving, a stream of witches hurtled downward.

They were coming straight toward me.

I scrambled to my feet. For a moment, I teetered on the limb. Then I lost my balance and fell into the center of the circle at Andelica's feet.

ACCIDENTAL WITCH

7

The shrieking and howling ceased abruptly.

I looked up. A thicket of witches wrapped in dark swirling capes stood over me.

"What is it?"

"A girl!"

"What is she doing here?"

Their voices sounded like tin cans scraping together, like nails ripping across metal, like rusty pipes battering old walls.

This is the end, I thought. I'd stumbled once too often.

The witches' stiff capes snapped in the wind. Their eyes glared down at me. Their pointed hats looked like daggers.

Were they going to change me into a dragonfly . . .
or maybe a groundhog . . . or even a bumblebee?
Would it feel like an electric shock or like a bull-
dozer rolling over me?

I closed my eyes and waited.

I felt a feathery touch on my arms, I felt myself rising. I felt someone dusting me off.

I opened my eyes.

A tall gaunt witch with a gray ponytail took out an
embroidered black handkerchief and wiped my face.

"Call me Jacky," she whispered.

Andelica stood in front of me, beautiful and stern.
"Young Phoebe!"

Andelica knew my name!

"You're the one who spilled tea on me."

There was a murmur from the other witches.

"She spilled tea on a senior witch?"

"And now she falls into our circle!"

"Bad luck—for us!"

"This should not have happened," said a short
witch with bright red cheeks. "It's not a good time for
us to take on an apprentice. To say the least!"

"This is true, Mesmerelda," Andelica said. "But it's
too late now."

"Can't we just pulverize the little trespasser and
start over?" Mesmerelda said.

"Rules are rules," Andelica said sternly. "Like it or not, she's now one of us."

"Alas . . . ," Mesmerelda sighed.

"What's going on?" I asked. "Did I do something wrong?"

Andelica turned to me. "You were caught between the downward force of one hundred witches and the upward force of my spell. You absorbed some very concentrated powers."

"Huh?"

Andelica frowned. "Every twenty years or so, it happens. We have our records. Some girl blunders into witchhood and early powers."

"You mean I'm a—"

"Yes!"

"—witch?" I stammered. "You're not kidding? This is for real? I have powers?"

"And unfortunately for us, you can't give them back." Mesmerelda gave me a sharp jab with her elbow. "You're a witch now, all right, for better or worse. Probably worse."

Andelica traced a circle from the top of my forehead to my chin, then touched both my cheeks. "You are now a novice, twenty-third stage. As you fell, so shall you reap," she intoned.

I looked at Andelica, tall and regal—with the

power to summon hundreds of witches, appear in classrooms, and clean up disasters with a snap of her fingers.

Then I looked at myself, short and round—with nothing but the uncanny ability to fall out of trees at the worst possible moment. "I'm a witch?" I said again. "I have what it takes to be a witch of Sector Five?"

"Not really, not yet," Mesmerelda said. "Let's just say you were the wrong person at the right time."

"We'll give you some instructions and training, of course," Jacky said.

"Why should we?" Mesmerelda snapped. "She's an accidental witch. Why go out of our way for her?"

Andelica pulled a tiny leather-bound book out of her pocket, flipped it open, and read. "We are obliged to help train the accidental witch, whenever we can take time away from our duties."

"But this is our busy season!" Mesmerelda protested. "We have forests to seed, oceans to patrol, tornadoes to twist. We have plants to heal and story tapestries to weave! And I have my customers!"

"We'll all just have to do the best we can," Jacky said. She patted my back. "Poor thing! You arrived at the worst possible time. But that's the way the cobweb crumbles."

"I won't be any trouble!" I said. "Really! You can just help me whenever you're free."

I grabbed a branch of the tree and swung back and forth. "See? I'm strong and ready!" I lost my hold and tumbled to the ground. I jumped up. "Still ready!"

"Are we just going to let her loose?" Mesmerelda asked Andelica. "Look at her! Does she look like good witch material? This could get messy!"

The beautiful witch frowned.

"Powers are never predictable," she said. "Especially powers gained in this way. But young Phoebe is now one of us."

It was starting to sink in. "I really *am* a witch!" I danced around the clearing. "I am! I am! I've got magic!"

Jacky touched my shoulder. "Dear! Remember, start slowly. Be patient."

"Sure!" I agreed.

I grabbed a broom and wrapped my legs around it, as I had done so many times before in my kitchen. How hard could it be to learn to use a bunch of powers anyway? It couldn't be any harder than learning to ride a bike, could it?

"Whooo! Let's go!" I shouted.

And the broom moved! It made a rough scraping

noise as it swept across the ground. I saw myself flying above the rooftops waving to the crowds below.

Wouldn't Jennifer be impressed! She would stop talking about that stupid Mandy.

And Mandy would be so awestruck, for once she wouldn't have anything to say.

As for my Mom—now she'd start counting on me all the time. You can trust a witch.

The broom came to a halt. I hung in the air with my toes dangling above the witches' pointed hats.

Then, as fast as I'd risen, I dropped to the ground.

Mesmerelda snatched the broom away. "That's mine!" she said.

"Don't I get a broom?" I asked.

"Buy your own," she sniffed. "You novices expect everything to be given to you."

WITCHMART 8

The witches picked up their brooms. They were leaving!

"What about me?" I asked. "Where's my witch gear? Where's my official broom, cape, and hat? Where are you going?"

"We have business to attend to," said Mesmerelda. "Didn't you listen? It's our busy season. Customers are waiting for me!"

"Gotta fly, dearie," Jacky said. "See you round."

With a rustle of capes and a sweeping of brooms, the witches took off into the sky, all except Andelica. She pointed to her neon broom. "Hop on." I didn't even have time to get excited. With one powerful swoop, we were in the air. I clung to Andelica's waist. We were barely aloft, and then we were plummeting toward earth again so fast I thought we were going to crash. But Andelica landed us without even a jolt.

She was some driver. If she weren't a witch, she'd have been racing cars.

A warehouse stood directly before us. A large black-and-orange sign blinked on and off: Witchmart. Witchmart. Witchmart.

"You'll find everything you need there," Andelica said. "Hat, cape, and broom. Your broom will take you home when you're ready."

"It will? How?"

"Just talk to it!" Her broom rose into the air.

"Wait a minute!" I cried. "Andelica! Don't leave me alone!"

She plucked a bead from her glowing necklace and tossed it to me. It was cold and hard and seemed to shrink from my touch.

"What is it? What do I do with it?" I said.

"It's a calling bead," Andelica said. "Use it if you really need one of us. . . . So long!" She soared into the evening sky.

As I entered the building, a hearty voice boomed over a loudspeaker. "You are entering Witchmart, the most successful witch and warlock retailing store on the planet, outfitter to the stars, the moon, the sun. All of the modern witch's equipment in the latest styles at competitive prices.

"You'll find it all at Witchmart!"

Big yellow moon chandeliers cast ghastly lights over the aisles of merchandise. There were moaning boxes, ghostly sheets, plastic bats and toads, stacks of kitty litter, and row after row of brilliantly colored potions in large glass jars with dark stoppers, all tied with thick black ribbon.

"What can we do for you today?" It was the plump witch, Mesmerelda, with the red cheeks and the sharp elbows. "Oh, it's you," she said.

"I'm here for my first broom, hat, and cape," I said proudly.

"Come along! I don't have much time. I'm expecting a busload of important buyers from Pennsylvania." Mesmerelda steered me to a revolving rack of capes. There were flowing silken ones with red embroidered linings; cotton ones with flowers ("For the Demure Witch"); and black net capes for hot mosquito-filled days.

I pulled out a deep velvet cape, with a black swirling pattern imprinted on the fabric. "I like this one."

She snatched the velvet cape from my hands. "Those are designer capes. Not for you!" She pulled a shrunken, puckered nylon cape out of a cardboard box. It had a tear in the lining, and the black had faded.

It looked like somebody's leftover Count Dracula

cape that had been worn for fifteen Halloweens.

"This is what you can have," Mesmerelda said.

"This is it?"

I looked at the price tag. It had been marked down from $13.13 to $11.11, then to $7.77, $3.33, and final markdown, $1.13. Well, it was cheap enough, anyway.

Mesmerelda began pulling out dusty black hats from another cardboard box. "These are last year's models. Maybe we can find one to fit your head."

The first hat came down to my nose. "I can't see out of this. How am I supposed to steer my broom? Don't you have any smaller lightweight models?"

She plopped something that looked like an old dunce cap on my head.

Dust and spiders spilled over my face. The hat smelled like a musty suitcase and felt as heavy as one, too.

"Perfect," the witch said.

"Aaaachooo!"

She dragged me down another aisle.

"Aaaachooo!"

Did witches sneeze?

She yanked me around the corner, and there were the brooms—more brooms than I had ever seen. Some of them had designs tattooed on their sticks; others were wrapped in green and black ribbons;

some even had plaited straw. They were humming and stirring, buzzing and whirring. A few of them were banging against the wall.

I stared longingly at a turbo-powered broom, black cats tattooed on its stick, that was straining at its bonds.

"Don't even think about it!" The witch strode to the end of the display and pulled out a small puny broom. The tag said, "For beginners only. Low speed. Low altitude. Day trips only."

She pulled a small black calculator out of a deep pocket at the side of her cape. "That will be $99.13."

"What!" I held up the greasy shriveled cape. "This was marked down to $1.13. The cap was $3.37. The broom was $5.59. How does that make $99.13?"

"Witch math," Mesmerelda snapped.

I reached into my pocket. "I only have $2.55 left from my allowance."

"You can't buy the merchandise, then." She sounded pleased about it.

"That's not fair," I said. "I'm a witch. I need those things."

"You have to earn them," Mesmerelda said. "I did."

I noticed a book with a shiny green cover, the color of money, on a rack loaded with copies of *Witch Weekly* and *Witch Watch*. I opened it. Right on the first page, I read, "How to attract money in five easy spells. Suitable for beginners and slow learners. Quick results guaranteed."

"This is for me!" I said. Page one had three words in bold type: **"Think of money."**

That was easy. I thought of dollar bills, nickels, dimes, my allowance (a nice crisp new five), play money, real money, chocolate coins wrapped in gold.

Page two said: **"Think harder and bigger."**

I concentrated on piles of gold. Gold fillings in teeth, gold chains around necks, and gold rings on fat pinkies. I thought of King Midas's hoard, the pot of gold at the end of the rainbow, and gold bars at the Federal Reserve.

But still no money appeared.

Page three: **"Say the following words three times very fast: Gold coins, green bills, give me lots of them."**

It didn't even rhyme! What kind of a spell was that? Besides, I only wanted enough to pay for the cape, hat, and broom. Still, it was worth a try.

"Gold coins, green bills . . . ," I said.

The floor rumbled and rolled under my feet.

"Give me lots of them."

Spiders rained from the ceiling.

"Gold coins, green bills," I repeated again.

Fake warts and long teeth tumbled from the shelves. The air was thick with colored vapors. Five ghosts careened past the checkout counter.

I heard a low growling noise like thunder. Maybe that was the sound of . . . money!

"It's working! It's working!" I shrieked. Chandeliers crashed to the floor. A wall bulged and cracked. "Well, sort of."

"My store! My store!" Mesmerelda cried, her cheeks flaming red. "What are you doing?"

"I just tried a spell . . . ," I began.

"Take your things and *get out!*"

I threw the *Easy Money Spells* book on the counter, grabbed the hat, broom, and cape, and ran out the door.

A thundering rumble split the sky. A pink sulfurous cloud engulfed Witchmart. When the cloud lifted, the store was gone.

Was this what my powers could do? "I did theeaaaat . . . ?" Somehow I couldn't talk right. It felt as if there were a couple of bats flying around in my throat.

"My store!" Mesmerelda jabbed at me with her elbows. "What did you do with my store?"

I looked at her, then at the bare spot where Witchmart had been. A cloud of dust hovered over the ground.

"Maybe it relocated," I said.

BEGINNER'S BROOM

I looked around. Only a pile of dust where Witchmart had been. Mesmerelda had flown off in a huff. Not another witch in sight. No one but me and my broom.

I eyed it nervously. Would it be able to hold me? I wouldn't want it to sag or break in midair.

Then I thought of something else. Did witches' brooms have an intelligence of their own? I hoped so! This one needed to know how to get me home. Because I didn't.

The broom didn't look very smart. It was skinny and short.

Oh, well. I settled my hat on my head, threw my cape over my shoulder, and put one leg over the broom handle.

"Take me home," I said. "Okay?"

The broom didn't budge.

Maybe I needed a spell to ride it.

"Broom, vroom, sweep through the sky. Let me see if you can fly. . . ."

The broom twitched. We lifted a few inches off the ground and turned slowly in circles.

"Straight," I said. "Go straight as an arrow, straight as a stick. . . ."

The broom skimmed straight along the ground. Daisies brushed my ankles and chipmunks scampered out of the way.

"High! Fly high! To the sky!" I sounded like a first-grade reader. "Don't be shy."

We rocketed up.

"I'm going up!" I shouted. My nylon cape flapped around my shoulders. I gripped the broomstick tightly as it whirled me into space.

The clouds danced by us. Trees were just a memory. The earth below looked like a giant green beach ball.

The broom did have an intelligence of its own—and a mind of its own as well. It obeyed me only once—when I told it not to be shy. After that it didn't listen anymore.

With a whiz and a bang and a zoom, it headed straight for a sullen little cloud.

Going through a cloud is a different experience from looking at a cloud. From the ground, clouds are puffy and wispy and dry and cuddly looking. When you're inside one, you find out that they are wet. And clingy. And cold.

Drops of moisture dripped from my hat into my eyes. My cape clung limply to my back.

The broom somersaulted in and out of clouds like a stunt diver off a springboard.

"Whoooa!" I screamed, as the broom hurtled through the sky. My stomach leaped and plunged with every new dive.

"Stop! Halt! Cease! Desist! *Please* slow down!"

It tore through yet another cloud.

I begged it not to go any higher. It ignored me.

I pleaded with it to have pity. It didn't.

"Do you speak English!" I shrieked. "*Arrêtez!* . . . Opstay! Catfeathers! Broomcackle! Heeeeelllllllpppp!"

This was a beginner's broom? This *was* a beginner's broom! I had bought a young untamed broom. A green, wild, dizzy broom.

"Down!" I ordered. The broom did a series of wild flip-flops. I cried for my mother.

We plunged earthward. We were heading straight for a tree.

Visions of broken arms and legs flashed in my mind. "Up, up!" I screamed.

If the broom had had brakes, they would have screeched. We barely cleared the tree. My feet tore through the leaves. Birds shot up around me.

I started to breathe a sigh of relief. Too soon!

Now it was flying low—and wild. We caused three drivers to go off the road and narrowly missed two head-on collisions.

When we brushed against a power line, the broom's straw flared, but it thought fast. It dove toward the earth and dipped itself in a pond to put out the flames. Of course, I got drenched, too.

Then the broom had the bright idea of going *through* a barn rather than over it. I came out sneezing and covered with hay.

At last I saw my house. "We're here! Stop! We're home!"

But the broom had to have one final fling.

It whirled around the roof, driving fat gray pigeons into the air. For a moment, I thought we were going down the chimney. Then the broom thought better of it and headed for my bedroom window.

As we flew through the window, the tinkle of breaking glass sounded gently behind me. I tumbled off the broom and landed in a heap on the floor.

THE IDEAS KIDS GET

10

I lay facedown on the bedroom rug, breathing in the delicious aroma of dust and bedsprings. My witch's cap had rolled off my head, my cape had twisted itself around my legs, and my bedroom window was in pieces over the floor.

More shattered glass. The second time this week.

Wait till my mother saw that.

I wiggled my fingers and toes, flexed my knees, and turned my head to the right and left. Everything still worked.

I felt as if I had been away from home for at least two days. But the clock on the wall said 8:01 P.M. I had only been gone for twenty minutes.

More witch magic?

I looked around for my broom.

It leaned against my bedroom wall at a jaunty angle, looking very pleased with itself.

I shook my finger at it. "Don't ever take me on a ride like that again!"

It slunk toward the closet, pouting.

"Bee? Bee!" My mother was coming up the stairs. "Is that you, dear? I thought I heard glass breaking."

She pushed open the door and stared at my broken window and then at me. "Phoebe! Are you all right? What happened?"

This didn't seem like exactly the right moment to say, "Guess what, Mom, I'm a witch!"

"You see, it was like this . . . ," I began. "I had a little crash, er, an accident, Mom."

"I don't understand. What are you doing on the floor?"

"The floor feels so good," I said. "The earth beneath my feet. Good old terra firma . . ."

"And *what* are you wearing, Phoebe?"

"Witch's garb," I said shyly, but proudly.

"Halloween is five months away!"

"This isn't a costume, Mom. This is for real." I stood up and took a deep breath. "I'm a witch, Mom. With powers and everything."

"I've never heard of a ten-year-old witch before."

Her eyes slowly moved from me to the window. "Bee. What happened this time? You can tell me."

"I flew through the window."

My mother again took in everything: the ratty cape, the oversize hat, the broken window. Then she shook her head sadly.

"I'm an accidental witch," I said. "Me—your daughter. I'm the first accidental witch in twenty years!"

"Accidental for sure—witch, never!" said my mother. "Not in a hundred years." She took the broom and began sweeping glass fragments into a pile. "This is not what a witch does, Bee."

"Mom, that's my witch's broom!"

She held it away from her. "It looks like a plain ordinary broom to me, Phoebe."

She felt my forehead, checked my pulse, and made me stick out my tongue and say "Aaah" three times. "Did you eat or drink anything unusual tonight, dear?" she said.

"I'm fine, Mom. Like I said, I'm just a witch."

"The ideas that kids get," she sighed.

The ideas that parents *didn't* get, I thought.

JUMP-START
YOUR POWERS

My career as a witch was not off to a brilliant start.

But all was not doom and gloom.

I had flown twice and made a store disappear. I had a broom, a cape, a hat, and a calling bead. Of course, I still didn't know how to operate any of my equipment, but that was a minor detail that I would soon clear up.

But first I had to get the rest of the glass off the floor.

I picked up the broom and began to sweep.

That broom wasn't much better at sweeping than it was at flying. It kept knocking the fragments of glass across the room.

Now that I was a witch, I probably shouldn't have been sweeping at all.

I decided to restore the window through the strength of my powers. It would not only save a lot of allowance money but might also convince my mother I really was a witch.

I took a deep breath, crossed my fingers, and concentrated on getting the glass back into the window. Nothing happened. The glass still lay all over the floor.

I waved my hand. I wriggled my eyebrows. I pushed my belly button.

That didn't work, either.

I pulled out Andelica's calling bead. "How do you work?" I asked it. It didn't answer.

I breathed hard on it. It stared at me like a plastic eyeball.

Probably I needed a spell.

My eye fell on my old spelling book from second grade. I pulled it off the shelf and opened it.

"Spring thing ring," I chanted from page twenty-five. "Plant grant rant."

It didn't make any sense to me, and I guess it didn't make any sense to the calling bead or to my powers, either.

I tossed the book on the bed.

Maybe I didn't really have powers. Maybe I had just gotten a quick dose of witchhood that wore off after a few hours.

"I need help," I said.

Andelica's bead glowed lime green.

"That's more like it!" I rubbed it between my hands, and a piece of paper floated down from the ceiling.

On it, written in tiny letters, were the words, "Magic Lesson #1: Jump-start Your Powers."

Now we were getting somewhere. Or were we? The tiny letters kept leaping off the page. No matter how fast I grabbed, I couldn't catch another word.

Maybe what I had to do was jump. That was easy.

I kicked off my shoes, climbed on my bed, and jumped. High. High. Higher!

"Wheeee! It's fun to be a witch!"

I waved my arms. My big black cape billowed out behind me.

Another paper fluttered down from the ceiling.

Congratulations, Phoebe, you have jump-started your powers.
You may now use them as you please, but please—use caution and remember . . .
you are an accidental witch.

*Magic Lesson #2: Remember, Only Use
the Calling Bead for Emergencies!
or you'll be sorry*

Words began to pop into my head. "Wacky weird witches' powers!" I chanted, "Mend the broken glass.

"Wonderful wild witches' towers . . . Let's fix it fast!"

I jumped higher and higher. My head grazed the ceiling. A humming sea-colored light filled the room. It gathered itself together into a ball. It shimmered and shook like sea green jello.

"Whaaat?" I opened my mouth in astonishment, and the humming sea-colored light slid down my throat like a dose of medicine.

My hands and feet got hot. My face was ice cold.

I pointed my finger at the broken glass. "Shattered glass and broken bits, come together, prove my witch's wits!"

The tiny pieces of glass flew to the windowpane and locked themselves in place.

But the window was still cracked. It looked like a piece of ice someone had stepped on.

"Smooth! Smooth! Smooth that groove!"

Slowly the glass began to melt. The sharp edges dissolved.

"That's good," I approved.

The glass began to blow out like a giant piece of bubble gum.

"Hey, what's happening?"

It swelled bigger and bigger.

"Stop!" I yelled, but too late. With a huge *pop!* the window exploded.

My mother came running up the stairs. "What was that noise?"

I stood in front of the open window, trying to look casual. The frame was still hot and sticky from the molten glass. "Mom, no glass on the floor!" I said.

I just hoped she didn't look down into the yard, where the glass was hanging in long drippy strands like Christmas icicles from every plant and bush.

My mother got down on her hands and knees to check the floor. Then she inspected under the bed and inside the closet.

She stood up and dusted off her hands. "You've done an excellent job of cleaning that glass from the floor, Bee. You won't get any splinters. And I like the way you've scraped the window frame clean. Very thoughtful."

"Sure, Mom. You can count on me."

Now all I had to do was clean up the glass icicles before she saw them. This magic business was complicated!

I got up early the next morning, collected all the icicles from the bushes and raked the last pieces of glass out of the grass.

My mother stuck her head out the window. "Yard work before school? Bee, what's gotten into you?"

"A few witches' powers, Mom, nothing more."

"Did you say you wanted marshmallow Cocoa Puffs for breakfast? We're all out of it!"

If she didn't learn that I was a witch soon, we were going to have a lot of misunderstandings.

12
IT FOLLOWED ME
TO SCHOOL ONE DAY

Have you ever had a broom follow you to school?

I was halfway down the block when I realized it was following me. "Go back!" I said. "Go back home!"

Unfortunately, a witch's broom is not like a dog. You can't order it home or to sit and beg. It won't fetch sticks, either.

"Feeeeebeeee!" It was Mandy, coming down the hill.

And Jennifer was trailing behind her.

"What's the broom for?" Jennifer asked.

"So she can sweep up anything she spills!" Mandy burst into loud laughter.

I drew myself up. "This happens to be a witch's broom."

"What did you do, steal it?"

"I've been initiated as a witch of Sector Five," I said proudly.

Mandy poked Jennifer. "Did you hear that? *She* has been initiated. *She* is a witch. Her. Phoebe, the Bumbling Bee. She's taken up lying now!"

"Phoebe wouldn't lie," Jennifer said.

I flashed her a grateful look and then blurted, "I flew last night. Messages dropped from my ceiling. My window was like bubble gum. And this broom will do anything I tell it to do."

"Come on, Bee, we can't believe that," Jennifer said. "Didn't your mother buy that broom a few days ago?"

"I'm telling the truth, Jennifer. Watch this!" I dropped my books and flung my leg over the broom. "Let's go, Broomy."

The broom did not move.

"This is no time to get picky," I muttered. "Take me up!"

"Why are you doing this?" Jennifer asked.

"Beam her up, Broomy!" Mandy shouted.

I gave the broom a kick. "Up up *up!*"

"Maybe it needs fuel," Mandy said. "How

about a little tea?"

I shook the broom. "What's wrong with you?" I said. "Remember yesterday? Zoom, zoom? Sixty miles an hour in the sky?"

Mandy was poking Jennifer and grinning.

"Well, forget it!" I threw the broom on the sidewalk. It lay there like a dead thing.

I reached in my pocket and pulled out Andelica's bead. "This is a genuine witch's bead," I announced.

"Whoever heard of a witch's bead?" Mandy scoffed. "That thing looks like a dumb marble!"

"It does look like a marble," Jennifer echoed. "Is that the one you took from me last year?"

Mandy began to hum a popular tune from last spring. "You put a spell on me. . . ."

She linked arms with Jennifer. "You put a spell on me. . . ." Mandy continued to hum.

"Traitor, fink, betrayer," I muttered. Why did Jennifer have to like that awful Mandy so much? Why couldn't she be my witch-struck friend again?

"Spice, ice, and long-tailed mice . . . ," I chanted loudly, trying to drown them out. "Jars of jelly, rolls of deli . . ." I pointed my finger at Jennifer. "Make this friend mine again!"

A swarm of tiny blue arrows shot out of my fingers straight toward Jennifer.

She screamed and held up her math book as a shield.

The arrows bounced off and whizzed back at me.

I put out my hands to catch them, but they had other ideas. They dodged around my hands and hit me on the arms, chest, nose, and legs. It didn't hurt, just felt strange and tingly. And then they disappeared.

I was going to say something like, "That'll teach you to mess with a witch," or, "Ha, ha, I'm a witch and you're not," but what came out of my mouth was a pitiful, "Please, Jennifer, be my friend again."

I fell to my knees. "Please, please, please!" I clutched her ankles. "I will always be your faithful friend."

It was truly nauseating. But I couldn't stop myself. My magic words had turned back on me.

"Yuck," Jennifer said. "Get off."

"Step on her," Mandy said. She kicked my schoolbooks into the gutter.

"You got her books all wet," Jennifer remarked.

"If her books are wet, Witchy will dry them off. She can just snap her fingers."

I did. I snapped my fingers as hard as I could, wishing I could make her disappear, too.

Nothing happened. My books were still wet. And Mandy and Jennifer walked off together.

Jennifer didn't even look back.

The broom lay limply on the ground. "I haven't forgotten you," I said. "Though I wish I had. . . . Dirt pebbles, mouse sticks. Mushroom crumbles, house snicks! Once and for all, *go home!*"

The broom jumped up, swept a few leaves off the sidewalk, then flopped over again.

I picked up my books, stuck the broom under my arm, and carried it back home. I taped it to the end of my bed with extra strong packing tape.

"Don't you dare get into any mischief while I'm gone!" I said in my sternest voice. "Or you'll be sorry."

The broom's bristles drooped. It looked absolutely pcnitent.

Obviously, you had to get tough with this broom.

BUBBLE TROUBLE

13

I ran all the way to school, but I was still late.

As I opened the door to the classroom, Mr. Belkey was reading from the history book.

He looked up. "Late, Phoebe?"

"Transportation problems," I mumbled.

Mandy smiled evilly.

Jennifer was sitting behind her. I waved vigorously at her, smiling so hard my face hurt.

Jennifer picked up her history book and hid behind it.

Mandy raised her hand.

"Yes, Mandy?"

"I want everybody to know," Mandy said in her

loudest voice, "Phoebe is now a witch."

Cheers, shouts, hurrahs, boos, whistles, hisses, and applause.

Except for Peter Cook. He was staring at me in a thoughtful, interested way.

Mr. Belkey clapped his hands. "Quiet, class! Mandy, you know this is impossible. Phoebe cannot be a witch. You attended the presentation of the senior witch the other day."

"I saw Phoebe's broom this morning, Mr. Belkey. And her genuine witch's bead. I saw them with my own eyes."

"Really!" Mr. Belkey said.

Mandy trained her Apple-bright smile on him. "Yes! And since we've studied witches, I think Phoebe should give us a demonstration."

"Yeah!" the class yelled.

Mr. Belkey looked stern. "This is not part of today's lesson plan."

I nodded my head in agreement. Sure, I wanted everyone to know I was a witch. But I didn't want to make a fool of myself in front of the entire class.

"Please, Mr. Belkey, please?" Mandy pleaded.

"Please," the class echoed.

"Since everyone feels so strongly, Phoebe may give us a short demonstration."

"I don't feel so strongly, Mr. Belkey," I said.

"Come up here, Phoebe. Don't be shy. Mandy, will you assist Phoebe in this demonstration?"

Mandy sauntered to the front of the room. I stumbled after her. "Come *on*, witch," she said. "Show us your stuff."

What stuff? Was she talking about my uncooperative broom or my unreliable spells?

I tried to concentrate. All I could think of were Mandy's sneering words. That wasn't helping me any.

"If I was your mother," I hissed, "I'd wash your mouth out with soap, you wormy Apple!"

Soap bubbles—big fat shiny ones—began to foam out of Mandy's mouth.

The class gasped in amazement.

I was as surprised as everyone else.

I hadn't felt my powers rising in me. But then I hadn't expected to. I figured that they were home catnapping or chatting with the broom.

Bubbles gushed out of Mandy's open mouth, over her chin, and down the front of her purple shirt.

She was spurting bubbles like a fountain.

"Now, young ladies!" Mr. Belkey came toward us, pink and sputtering. "Enough of this spitting. Mandy, I'm surprised at you!"

Mandy cast me a look of pure hatred. "Gttt me outta dssss," she gurgled.

"So unsanitary," Mr. Belkey said. "Go clean your-selves up!" He stamped his foot and hit a patch of wet soapy goo.

"Eeeekkkkk!" he cried, as he went sliding across the floor.

I ran for the door, with Mandy following.

The bubbles were coming out of her mouth in torrents now. The floor was covered with bubbly, slippery goo.

"Bub . . . bub . . . bub . . . ," Mandy cried.

The sixth-grade gym class marched past in crisp blue uniforms.

I waved my hands frantically to warn them.

The class kept marching, heads high, arms swing-ing. Then they hit the floor, scattering like bowling pins.

"Stppp issss!" Mandy shrieked, splattering my face.

"Abracadabra?" I tried. "No. Hocus pocus. Jiminy cricket? Soap, soap, go away . . ."

Nothing worked. The more I talked, the faster the bubbles poured out of Mandy's mouth.

My jeans were wet to the knees. The sixth graders' hair hung in sticky clumps, and their gym suits clung dripping to their skin.

If I didn't do something fast, the school would be one giant bubble bath.

I searched in my pockets for another sheet of instructions, a spelling book, anything. What I came up with was the witch's bead. That note that fluttered down from the ceiling had said for emergency use only.

This was definitely an emergency.

I rolled the bead between my palms.

"Andelica!" I cried. "Help!"

A path parted in the bubbles, and Andelica strode majestically toward us like a witch from the sea, her long black hair flowing down her back.

"Toadfeathers, marshmallows, broomflies! What is this?" she asked sternly.

"Spppttt!" Mandy said, pointing at me.

I shrugged modestly. "I did this, Andelica, but I'm not sure how to stop it."

The sixth graders raised their heads and stared with mouths open.

Andelica waved her hand. *Bubbles and troubles; high and low; soap and clean scent; fly and grow.*

I heard a loud *crack*! The soap and goo vanished into the palm of Andelica's hand as though a vacuum cleaner had sucked it up.

"Thank you, Your Grace," Mandy breathed, bowing low.

I grabbed a piece of paper and a pencil from my pocket and started to write down the spell. "Bubbles, gubbles; high and show . . ."

"Would you repeat that spell, please?" I asked.

"No!" Andelica said.

"Why not?"

"Why not!" She drew herself up. "You are not ready for a powerful spell like that!"

"But I made the bubbles happen," I said. "Shouldn't I be able to make them disappear?"

"Not yet! Be patient!"

"I am," I said. "I'm patient, Andelica. Really, I am. It's just that I can never make my powers do what I want them to do."

"No doubt," Andelica said. "How long have you had them? Two days? What's two days, young Phoebe?" She snapped her fingers. "The flicker of a bat's wing. A wink of a cat's tail. Nothing."

"Huh?"

"You need a great deal of instruction to become a proper witch. Unfortunately for all of us, you're going to be on your own more than is good for you. You'll have to learn by trial and error. Unavoidable, but lamentable."

I nodded. I wasn't sure about the trial part, but I'd sure been making plenty of errors.

Mandy had been listening to our conversation. She shoved me aside and planted herself in front of Andelica. "You mean *Phoebe's* a witch? You must be joking." Mandy laughed shrilly. "I refuse to believe it."

Andelica gazed steadily at Mandy.

"Why is she a witch and I'm not?" Mandy demanded. Her voice rose higher. "I want an explanation! Now!"

The beads on Andelica's necklace were slowly turning dark red.

I nudged Mandy. "I wouldn't push it if I were you. . . ."

Andelica's necklace looked hot enough to explode.

"It's not fair!" Mandy screamed.

"Quiet!" Andelica roared. Green and orange flames leaped up the wall, then disappeared without leaving a single charred surface.

The sixth graders cowered in a dark corner.

Mandy had gone pale as a green apple. Her mouth was open, but not a sound came out.

"That was great, Andelica," I said. "No one has ever shut up Mandy before. If you don't ever show me another spell, I'd like to know how you did that one."

The witch turned her fierce gaze on me.

"Never mind," I said. "Just kidding."

The witch muttered to herself. It sounded like,

"Why me? Why me?"

She tapped the center of my forehead. A pale gray light wiggled down to my toes.

"Today's magic will have no results," Andelica snapped. "The memory of your spells will fade from the minds of those who witness them."

"You mean no one will remember the bubbles coming out of Mandy's mouth? Not Jennifer? Not Peter? Not even Mandy?" I protested. "How will anyone know I'm a witch?"

"They won't. They can't. They don't need to. Your magic went too far."

"But . . ." I was about to say, "No fair!" then thought better of it.

The witch snapped her fingers, and her neon broom flew smartly to her side.

Not like some other brooms I could mention.

"I have to go now," she said. "You called me away from a mud slide just west of here. And now I'm going to be late for the story weaving afterward."

"Well, good-bye," I started to say, but Andelica was already gone.

And Mandy and I were sitting in class again.

"See?" I whispered to Jennifer. "Now do you believe I'm a witch?"

"I don't know what you're talking about, Bee."

At least she didn't look disgusted anymore. And I wasn't on my hands and knees proclaiming eternal devotion.

Andelica had canceled that spell, too.

MY INCREDIBLE
DISAPPEARING MAGIC

At lunch, I decided to fill my glass with water without leaving the table.

"Watch this," I said to Jennifer, who was sitting opposite me.

I snapped my fingers. My glass filled with water.

I smiled triumphantly. "You see, Jennifer. That is how a witch does it."

"A who does what?" Jennifer said.

"Don't pretend you don't know." I lifted the glass to my lips. It was empty.

"You're drinking *air*!" Jennifer screeched.

Then Andelica's words came back to me: "Today's magic will have no results."

"Mmm," I said, thinking fast. "Fresh air. Delicious drink."

"Bee, you are getting weirder all the time." Jennifer picked up her tray and set it down at Mandy's table.

*   *   *

Then there was gym class.

"Up the ropes we go," the gym teacher said, as I walked into the gymnasium.

Just my luck. The ropes. I could never get past the knot at the bottom.

"Hey, Stumble Bee," Mandy called. She was practically on the ceiling. The Apples were oohing and aahing. "Come on up. The view is fine."

"No thanks." I wished we were doing something nice and safe—like square dancing or miniature golf.

"Are you *afraid*?"

The Apples tittered.

"Of course not."

"She's afraid," Mandy said. She hung by one hand. Show-off.

I would show her.

I ran to the rope. My powers were fizzing inside me. I felt like root beer in a can that someone had shaken hard.

Usually the rope burned the palms of my hands and my fingers. But today it felt like velvet.

My arms and legs gripped the rope, and up I

whizzed, easy as could be, until I was directly across from Mandy.

"Hey, Mandy. The view *is* fine." I tried not to think about how high I was or how hard the shiny wooden floor below.

Mandy gaped.

Then I slid down, easy as could be.

I looked up at her. "You see?"

"See what?" She thumbed her nose at me.

"Up the ropes we go," the gym teacher said. "Just give it a try, Phoebe."

"But I did!"

"Now, now, Phoebe, you can try a little harder than that. One of these days you'll make it up a foot or two," she said encouragingly.

The memory of your spells will fade in the minds of those who witness them. . . .

Oh, well. At least *I* remembered. Andelica hadn't wiped out my memory.

*   *   *

After school, I waited around for Jennifer, but she never showed up.

I was halfway home when Peter Cook caught up with me. "Hi, Bee," he said.

"Hi, Peter."

"Going home?"

"Uh-huh," I said. "Are you?"

"Uh-huh."

We stared at each other.

"Strange," he said, at last.

"What?"

"School today."

"School today was strange?"

He nodded. "Definitely."

"Definitely?"

"My clothes smell like bubble bath. I can't figure out why. For some reason, I thought you might have something to do with it, Phoebe."

I was so surprised I crashed into him. Hadn't Andelica's spell erased his memory?

"You just stepped on my toes," Peter said.

"Oh! Sorry."

"That's okay. It's just toes." He sniffed the sleeve of his shirt. "Bubble bath. Definitely," he repeated.

"Well, as a matter of fact—," I began.

Just then a bus roared past, filled with witches pointing their fingers at us.

"Did you see that?" I said.

"What?" Peter said.

"That bus."

"What bus?"

"It had witches in it."

"Witches? Oh, Phoebe!"

"Oh, never mind! Anyway, to answer your question—"

"What question?"

"You know, about the bubble bath . . ."

"Bubble bath?"

"You said you noticed something different in school today."

Peter looked perplexed. "The usual boring stuff."

"Well, what about me? I don't seem any different to you?" I said hopefully.

"Of course not! You're the same old Bee."

I sighed. Some invisible crack in Andelica's spell had just been repaired by a busload of witches.

MOTHER-DAUGHTER CHAT

15

After school, I had to vacuum the living room. As I pulled the cleaner out of the closet, I grumbled, "I wish you'd do this job yourself."

Good idea! One of my best. I waved my hand over the machine and intoned, "Dust, rust, and bits of broom. Go, and vacuum the living room."

It did.

It zoomed around, cleaned the rug and the floor, wrapped its own cord, and put itself away in the closet. It was all done in less than a minute. My powers were back!

I went into the kitchen to tell my mother the living room was clean. She was standing by the stove, stirring a pot. "How was school, dear?" she asked.

"Clean," I answered.

"Speaking of clean, don't forget the vacuuming."

"All done, Mom."

"You just came in. You couldn't possibly have vacuumed the whole living room."

"I did it, Mom! I told you, I'm a witch. I used my powers!"

My mother stirred harder.

"Phoebe . . ." Her voice was tense. "We need to have a little mother-daughter chat. We're going too far with this witch business, aren't we?"

"It's been going a little fast, but I don't think it's too far," I answered.

I glanced at her face. Time to change the subject. "What's for dinner, Mom?"

"Spaghetti surprise."

"Oh no. Not that stuff again!"

"What's wrong with spaghetti surprise? I thought you liked it. That's why I made it."

"Oh, Mom. It looks like worms, it tastes like worms, it acts like worms! Squirmy little wormies!"

I leaned over to look into the pot, and there they were! Hundreds of worms writhing in a bubbling red sea.

"Mom! Worms! You're serving us worms for supper!"

"Phoebe, this is not a very funny joke."

"No joke, Mom! Don't worry, I'll take care of it for you."

I picked up the pot and emptied it over the back porch railing. The worms hit the ground with a burst of pink smoke that smelled like old socks.

When I returned to the kitchen, my mother was filling a kettle with water.

"It's all right, Mom. I got rid of them."

"Got rid of what, dear?"

"The worms."

"What worms?"

"The worms in the spaghetti, Mom!"

"Worms in the spaghetti?" my mother said. "What a sense of humor, Bee! Just like your father!"

"Ha-ha," I said.

Andelica's memory-erasing spell was still working.

I would probably have to vacuum the living room again, too.

"Guess what," my mother said. "I'm making spaghetti surprise for supper tonight. Your favorite!"

"Oh, great, Mom," I said, thinking fast. "Thanks a lot, but no appetite."

In my room, I took out my science homework. Frog anatomy. I had to draw lots of pictures of frogs' legs and heads and stomachs. Lots of details. Lots of work.

Wait—did I really have to do all that work?

Didn't witches know everything about frogs? Yes.

Didn't they use them in potions and brews? Yes.

Didn't they change enemies into frogs? Yes.

Couldn't a witch use her powers to do frog home-work? Yes! Yes, yes!

First step: Put pen, blank paper, and science book on desk.

Second step: Wave hand in the air.

Third step: Concentrate hard.

Fourth step: Concentrate on frogs.

Fifth step: Concentrate on frogs leaping through the air.

Result: Book leaps into air.

That was a start, though not exactly what I had in mind.

Suddenly the pen joined the book near the ceiling and started chasing it. Then the book turned and started chasing the pen. They were having a game of hide-and-seek, darting in and out of my mobile of the planets.

"Bee . . . Can I come in?" my mother called. "You must be hungry by now. I brought you a bowl of spaghetti surprise," she said, opening the door.

Oh no. "Thanks, Mom, that's great," I said.

She put the tray down on my desk and picked

up my homework paper.

"Tonight's homework. Haven't really started it yet, Mom—"

"'Apple cherry toad pie,'" she read aloud. "'Add three toads to a pile of cherry pits and apple peelings. Mix well. Say spell. Pour batter. Get fatter.' Phoebe! What class is this for?"

My magic! It had done my homework—sort of.

"I didn't write that, Mom. But I made it happen. I've been trying to tell you, I really am a witch. It's official, and I can do magic." I pointed to the ceiling where the book and the pen were still playing hide-and-seek. "Look. I did that, too."

My mother looked up. "What did you do?"

The book and the pen had disappeared. Something else for me to worry about.

"I know you've always wanted to be a witch, Bee, but you have to be realistic. We've never had a witch in the family. Be sensible, dear! We've never even had witches as friends. . . . You have to keep your feet planted solidly on the earth."

Well, that's why I had the broom taped to the bed.

"Think of the life witches lead, Bee. Out at all hours in all kinds of weather. And the heights! Those rickety brooms. No seat belts!"

She took my hand. "I don't want to hurt you, dear, but it's time you faced up to facts. You are

78

not witch material. Very few girls are. I can remember only a handful from this town who have become witches, Phoebe, and all of them were at least fourteen when they apprenticed. Besides, there were witches in most of their families, and they were brought up to it."

"But, Mom . . ."

"You know," my mother said. "We have something in common, Bee. When I was a little girl, I wanted to be an astronaut."

"Oh, Mom."

"We both, you and I, have dreamed of flying."

"I *can* fly."

"This is just pretend, isn't it, Phoebe?"

"My witch's cape, Mom! My hat! My broom!" I pointed to the broom taped to my bed. "See that? It's a witch's broom."

"I *know* you're teasing me, Phoebe. It's that wonderful imagination of yours."

"Mom! Didn't you ever want to be a witch?"

"Not me. I wasn't good enough."

"You weren't?" I had always thought my mother was good at everything.

"I didn't have any natural talent."

"But what if *I* do?"

"Someone would have noticed it," my mother said. "I would have. Mothers notice those things."

"Mom." I grabbed at her hand. "Maybe you missed it."

If my mother didn't believe me, who would?

"What's *really* bothering you, Phoebe? Is it those Apples again?"

"Oh, Mom. They always bother me."

"Is Mandy pushing you around?"

"Sort of. I make her foam at the mouth."

"This is why you want to be a witch, isn't it? So you can stand up to that snotty Mandy and her Apples."

I nodded. "You're right, Mom. I want to be a witch because . . . Mom! Don't confuse me. I already *am* a witch."

My mother shook her head and opened the door. "I hope that with a good night's sleep, Bee, you'll be back to yourself."

Ha! Fat chance of that. My life was getting more and more complicated. My mother didn't believe I was a witch. I was losing Jennifer, who'd been my only real friend. And my powers kept getting short-circuited.

I looked up and saw my science book and pen floating past the mobile. *Now* they showed up! Standing on a chair, I retrieved them, got a fresh piece of paper, and sat down to do my homework the hard way.

Actually, it was easier than using my powers.

ON TOP OF THE WORLD

When I woke the next morning, I was floating next to the ceiling.

My nose was bumping the light fixture, my pillow was bobbing in a corner, and my arm had gotten tangled in my mobile of the planets.

And this was just the start of the day.

"Bee? Are you up yet?" My mother was coming up the stairs.

"Just a minute!" How was I supposed to get down from the ceiling? I tried jumping, but my feet floated upward.

Was this the sort of problem witches faced in their daily lives?

Or was this just my weird, unpredictable, and plain

ornery powers acting up again?

I was starting to wish that I had become a witch at another time. Like five years from now, when I was older, smarter, more knowledgeable in every way. Then I might know what to do with these powers.

Looking on the bright side, if my mother saw me up here, maybe she'd finally believe I was a witch.

If Andelica's memory-loss spell wasn't still in force.

"Phoeeeebbbeee, I've got to get to work." The door opened. "I made you an extra big breakfast today. It's on the ta—"

My mother broke off in midword. "*What* are you doing on the ceiling?"

I smiled. "Just relaxing."

"Why are you relaxing on the ceiling?"

"That's where witches like to relax, Mom."

"No," my mother said. "No. I can't believe it. I *won't* believe it. My ten-year-old daughter is not a witch."

"Mom," I said. "Your ten-year-old daughter is a witch. Yes, it's true."

"No," my mother muttered. "There must be a logical explanation for this. Maybe you *hired* a witch to stage this? Or did you and Jennifer cook it up?"

"Mom—"

"No, never mind. Whatever it is you're going to say,

Bee, forget it. It's morning and time to get moving. So just come down right now. On the double."

"Okay, Mom," I said. "Sure thing." I concentrated on getting off the ceiling, but a kind of reverse gravity kept sucking me upward. The soles of my feet tingled. I was floating so high that my nose scraped the ceiling.

"Well, what's keeping you, Bee? Unbuckle yourself, unstrap yourself, unglue yourself, whatever it takes. I want you down and dressed in five minutes."

"I can't, Mom. You better go to work. I'll figure something out."

"And leave you on the ceiling?" My mother kicked off her shoes and climbed onto the bed. "All right, Phoebe. Don't worry. Mommy's here."

I stretched out my arms. My mother grabbed my wrists and pulled.

"What kind of glue did you use?" she asked. She tugged harder.

"Oow!" I cried.

"You can't spend the whole day on the ceiling," she said briskly. "There's school to go to and work to do."

"Toadpillows, marshpals, fluffadillies, get me off this ceiling before my arms fall off," I yelled. I heard a crunch and felt something loosening up.

"That's it! You're coming off," my mother said. "What did you do?"

"Nothing," I replied. And I was back on the ceiling again, stuck more firmly than ever.

"Toadpals, pillowdillies, fluffamarsh! Down, down, down!" I tried to repeat my spell, but the words came out wrong.

My mother grabbed me around the waist and hung on. "If we can't get you off, I'm going to have to call a carpenter! Or the fire department! Or a witch! We can't stay here all day."

"I wish I knew what to do," I said sadly. "I just want to get off this ceiling!"

As I uttered these words, down I went, landing on the bed, with my mother under me, still holding me tightly around the waist.

"I knew we could do it if we put our minds to it!" my mother said triumphantly. She untangled herself, brushed off her skirt, and stepped back into her shoes.

I rubbed my nose. It was sore from having bumped the ceiling so many times.

My mother glanced up at the ceiling and then at me. "I can't believe you went to all this trouble to convince me you're a witch."

"Mom," I said wearily. "I *am* a witch. I really am. Why don't you believe me?"

"Bee . . ." My mother was shaking her head. She looked like she was about to cry.

I wanted to say something comforting, make it up to her. I patted her cheek. "Don't worry, Mom. Be happy."

Too late, I realized what I had done.

A blissful smile formed on my mother's face. "What, me worry? I never worry. I'm not worried about *anything*. Never worry, that's my motto. Why, you just smile at that cute little Mandy, and you'll be best friends forever. Take my advice, little Bee. See how happy I am? You can be happy, too."

"Mom . . . ," I said.

My mother beamed at me. "If you want to pretend you're a witch, darling, and rig yourself up on the ceiling, I'm all for it. I need to be late for work once in a while, anyway. Life is so much fun when you're around, Bee."

Oh, help. Was this my mother?

"Bye-bye, sweet little Bee Bee!" My mother blew me a dozen kisses.

That was okay, but when she started skipping down the stairs and singing, "I'm Always Chasing Rainbows," I'd had it.

This had gone far enough!

"I want you back to normal," I yelled. "I want you to worry about me! Don't believe everything I say!"

Oh, what had I just said?

My mother stopped in midskip. She shook her head as if she had stepped into a lot of cobwebs.

"Are you still in your pajamas, Bee? Come *on*," she said. "Hurry up." She clapped her hands. "Let's get going! You don't have all day. How can you talk about being a witch, when you can't even get to school on time?"

I breathed a sigh of relief. My mom was back again.

FLOATING WORDS 17

A surprise quiz!" Mr. Belkey announced. "Myths and legends."

Usually, my favorite subject—next to witches, of course. But today it was hard to concentrate. My mind was racing.

What mean thing was Mandy going to say to me next? Was Jennifer going to speak to me *at all*? Maybe I'd sit with someone else for lunch.

Like Peter.

That wouldn't be so bad.

It was Peter who handed out the quiz sheets. "You probably know all the answers," he said, lingering by my desk for a moment.

I didn't want him to think I was conceited. "I don't know anything," I said.

"Ha!" Peter said. "I bet."

I shrugged modestly.

"Want to come over to my house after school?" he asked suddenly.

I glanced over at Jennifer. She was whispering to Mandy.

"Sure," I said. "I'd like to."

Peter's face brightened. "Great!" he said. He hurried to pass out the rest of the quizzes.

I flipped over the test sheet and stared at the first question. "Name three Greek goddesses." I knew I *should* know the answer, but I didn't.

I went to the next question. "Who found the Golden Fleece?" Another blank.

Everyone was scribbling answers. Except for me. I was scratching my head.

Then I realized what I had done. *"I don't know anything,"* I had said to Peter. I had emptied my mind like pouring water out of a cup.

"I need some answers!" I whispered. Letters appeared in the air. First an *l*, then a *u*, then an *e* and a *q* together. They shimmered and shone. They were like bubbles blown from a pipe.

I reached up and touched a *z*, then a *g*. More and

more letters flowed through the air. At first they came slowly, then faster and faster. Sentences and words streamed by my head.

I grabbed a handful and brought them down to my paper. "The telephone was invented by Alexander Graham Bell. . . . Pi equals 3.14. . . . The process by which leaves convert light into food is called photosynthesis. . . ."

They were answers all right, but not to the questions on the quiz.

"A sorry lot you are," I said. The words seemed to wilt right on the paper. "I need answers to *this* quiz."

Neatly written purple words appeared above me: Jason found the Golden Fleece. . . . Ceres, Minerva, and Aphrodite. . . . All right! Yes, these were the answers I needed.

But I had forgotten to ask for answers that would be mine alone.

Mandy stood up. "Mr. Belkey!" She scanned the classroom. "My answers are missing."

"Have they fallen behind your desk?"

"No! I checked already."

She marched over to my desk and peered at my paper. "There they are! Those are *my* answers!"

She kicked me—hard.

"Oow, Mandy!"

"What are you doing with Mandy's answers, Bee?" Jennifer asked.

I rubbed my leg. "Like I told you more than once, Jennifer, I'm a witch."

Jennifer shook her head sadly.

"I slept on the ceiling."

"Riiiight," Mandy said.

I ignored her. "I've changed spaghetti into worms, Jennifer."

"Can you change worms into spaghetti?" Mandy snickered. "Now give me back my answers, Slime Bee!"

"Oh, have them—who cares?" I said. The neat purple words snapped off my paper and headed toward Mandy's.

And I was staring once more at an empty paper.

"What are these words doing here?" Mr. Belkey called. There was a note of panic in his voice.

Mandy's answers had not returned to her. They were running wild in the classroom.

Stray words were everywhere—circling the globe, bumping against the ceiling, and dodging the wheel in the hamster's cage.

"Get out! Get out!" Mr. Belkey cried. He seemed to be a magnet for words. They buzzed like insects around his head. "Go away!"

He swatted at them. "Go away at once!" he ordered.

Words whizzed around his face, danced on his ears, and wrapped themselves around his neck like a scarf.

"Stop," I whispered. The words halted, wilted, dropped to the floor like dead flies.

Mr. Belkey brushed a few words from his plaid jacket. "Time's up, people!"

The magic was mine, but it wasn't helping me any. My paper was empty. I knew it was a zero. "I just wish these papers would disappear," I muttered.

They did. My paper disappeared. Everybody's paper disappeared.

Mr. Belkey looked dazed for a moment, but not for long. "You people think you're getting out of the quiz, but you're wrong. You're all going to have to take the quiz again," he said. "Right now!"

When Peter passed out the papers this time, I told him, "I know everything."

"I knew it," he said.

As I stared at the quiz questions, my mind swelled with knowledge. I knew about Greek mythology, but I also knew how to get crayon and grease stains out of polyester. I knew algebra, trigonometry, and how to cook soft-shelled crabs. I knew the history of the world and ten easy ways to build a bookshelf. I knew one hundred and twenty-seven train schedules and three epic poems in Old English.

There was so much information crowding my mind I couldn't find the quiz answers. When Mr. Belkey collected the papers, I still hadn't written a thing. Zero again.

"If I could only be normal again!" I said. The teeming in my brain subsided.

But "normal" was a joke. I hadn't been normal since I became a witch. My powers had gotten me into one mess after another. I was breaking windows, flooding hallways, and losing my best friend. I was failing tests, sleeping on the ceiling, and in danger of turning my mom into a happy zombie out of a TV commercial.

I couldn't walk or talk without magic exploding around me. Would I ever make these witches' powers work for me, not against me?

18
PETER DISAPPEARS

Peter Cook caught up with me outside the school. "Hi, Bee!"

I wiggled my hand at him in greeting. Since the test, I hadn't said very much. I was afraid of what might happen if I opened my mouth.

"Wait 'til you see my tree house!" Peter said. "I built it myself. Bet you didn't know I could do that!"

I shook my head. It was going to be hard to spend the afternoon at his house without saying a word. Maybe I could fake temporary paralysis of the vocal cords. Or a sore throat. Or something.

"We can eat supper up there!"

I tried to look excited while keeping my lips tightly pressed together.

"Right under the leaves. You can see all the

way across town, too."

I smiled at him. Peter didn't know me really well yet. Maybe he would just think I was the strong, silent type.

"How about that quiz?" Peter asked, after a short pause.

"Mmmm?"

"I think there was magic in it."

"Mmmhhfff?!"

Peter grabbed my arm. "You know what I've been thinking, Bee?"

I shook my head.

"You're a witch, aren't you?"

I nodded.

Peter's eyes brightened. "I've never had a witch for a friend before. What kinds of magic can you do?"

I clutched an imaginary broom and pantomimed riding in the sky.

"Wow."

I shrugged modestly.

"Anything else?"

"Uuuhh—mmmm . . ."

"Can you make me disappear?"

"What? No!"

"I bet you can. Make me invisible!"

"What for?" I said.

"It'll be fun!"

"It could be dangerous."

"I'm not scared," he said.

But maybe I was.

"We can talk to each other when someone walks by," Peter said. "They won't know what to think."

"Tricky," I muttered. "Who knows what could happen?"

Peter tugged at my sleeve. "Please? Please, Bee?"

"You really want to disappear, Peter? I don't even know if I can do it."

"Aww, Bee. I've never been so close to a witch before. Let's just try. Please . . ."

Just try? Could that hurt? And what if it worked? It might be fun to do something no ten year old had ever done before. Something magical and *wonderful*—for a change!

"Peter invisible, Peter divisible," I said, waving my hand in the air.

Nothing happened. Good thing, too. What if he'd suddenly divided up into ten pieces?

"Peter disappear, fade into the air," I tried again.

Peter's face and body glowed briefly, as if lit from within by a strange sun. Then the glow disappeared and he began to fade, as if he were a stain being washed out of the air.

"Peter, it's happening!"

"I know." His voice was hollow and strange.

And then he was gone—or at least his body was. I could still hear his voice, spooky and echoing.

"Wheee . . . Beee! I'm invisible!"

"Peter? Where are you?"

"Guess."

"Over here?" I groped in the air.

"No." I felt something feathery touching my arm, then my hair was being tugged gently from behind.

I whirled around. "Where are you?" I said again.

In reply, Peter tickled me under the chin.

I tried to catch hold of him, but he slipped away.

"Can't catch me!" he teased.

A woman walking her dog stopped and looked at me. "Who are you talking to, dear?"

"My invisible friend," I said.

"Aren't you a little old for that?"

Just then, a leaf floated up from the ground right in front of us. It danced around my head and then rested in midair.

The dog jumped up, barking. The woman yanked on the leash and hurried down the street.

"You scared her, Peter," I said. "Maybe I should bring you back."

"Do we have to?"

"We can't let this go on too long. Who knows what could happen?"

"Awww, I guess you're right."

"Anyway, your mother wouldn't like it if you came home invisible."

I paced back and forth on the sidewalk. "Peter back from dark and black . . ."

Nothing happened.

"Peter here, Peter gone; bring him back before the dawn . . ."

No, that wouldn't do—we wouldn't see him until tomorrow morning!

"Peter go, Peter come; bring him back before we get home . . ."

I gazed into the air. He was still invisible.

"How long does it take, Bee?"

"Don't worry, Peter. I'm working on it!"

How long *did* it take? What if I couldn't bring him back?

"Bee? Is everything okay?"

"Okay? Of course it is! Yes, Peter, be, be . . . patient!" I hoped I sounded more confident than I felt.

I found the witch's bead in my back pocket and rubbed it hard between my palms. "Help! Please! I need help!"

No beautiful witch appeared. Instead, a long scroll of paper fluttered down from the sky. I grabbed it and unrolled it. The scroll was black, completely dark, except for some words at the top that said: "Magic Lesson #3: Reversing an Invisibility Spell."

"Yes! That's what I need!" I shouted.

Words flashed like a comet across the page. "Reversing an invisibility spell is very difficult. Especially for an accidental witch. (We don't have to tell *you* that, do we?) Follow these instructions carefully and you will be able to retrieve anybody from the deepest invisibility. . . . A special note: you must be completely relaxed to learn the spell, or else you won't be able to remember it."

Relaxed! I was so tense that I almost didn't know my name anymore.

The page was empty for a moment, then more words appeared.

"Concentrate on the dark. . . . Just keep looking at the dark . . ."

I stared at the black paper. Tiny points of light appeared everywhere like stars coming out on a moonless night.

"Wow," I said.

The points of light danced in front of my eyes. I forgot about Mandy, I forgot about school and gym and tests and Jennifer. I even forgot about Peter. I just watched the lights, feeling peaceful and relaxed. Then I began to feel surges of energy, and suddenly I felt as if I could do anything.

More words flashed across the scroll: "Commit the following to memory immediately: Invisible boy! Come back to me. Appear again, so I can see. . . . Invisible boy, come back . . . come back . . . now, to me!"

I read the words seven times. Then a new message appeared on the scroll: "You are ready. As ready as an accidental witch can be."

"Okay," I said.

Then the dark scroll crumpled up and dissolved into ash just as if it had been thrown into a fire.

It was now or never. I took a deep breath and began to chant. "Invisible boy!" I said. Then I started again louder. "Come back to me. Appear again, so I can see. . . . Invisible boy, come back . . . come back . . . now, to me!" I yelled.

A hazy Peter-shaped cloud formed in front of me.

First an arm emerged. Then a leg. Then another arm. Then his feet emerged from the mist.

The cloud thinned. Peter stood grinning on the sidewalk in front of me.

I looked him over quickly for lost parts. "Well, you're all here," I said. "Thank goodness!"

"Beeee . . ." His voice was different—like a spider squeak.

"Peter? Do you feel okay?"

"I feel great!" he squeaked. "That was wonderful!"

"You're *really* okay?"

He shook his arms, then his legs. He wiggled his fingers and stuck out his tongue.

"It all works," he said. "Except for my voice." He sounded like a spider with a sore throat.

I studied him anxiously. "What will your mother say when she hears you talk?"

"Laryngitis," he said. "I get it all the time. Come on, let's go to the tree house."

"Peter? I need to go home." Suddenly I felt wobbly from head to toe. "I'm really tired. All that magic—"

"Sure," Peter squeaked. "Go home and rest. You can see the tree house another time."

"If your voice doesn't come back by tomorrow, give me a call."

Not that I knew what to do about it. I'd probably make it worse. He'd sound like a cricket—or an elephant—after I was through with him.

"Okay," Peter squeaked. "Okay."

I watched him skip down the street until he disappeared around the corner. Then I turned and staggered home.

POWERS FOR SALE:
NO REASONABLE OFFER
REFUSED

My hands were trembling, my feet were tottering, I was shaking all over. It felt like someone was pouring buckets of cold water from the top of my head to the bottom of my spine. Another close call! I had almost lost Peter. And maybe I'd lost his voice.

As if things weren't bad enough, just then my cape, hat, and broom decided to put on a show. The broom was knocking itself silly against the bedpost. The cape and hat marched out of the closet and around my room.

"What's the matter with you?" I cried. "Don't you know how to behave in someone's house?"

Suddenly there was a crash. The broom had burst free, whirled past my desk, swept everything onto the floor, knocked over a lamp, and was now tangling with the curtains.

"Cool it!" I yelled.

The hat and cape began to dance together.

"This is it!" I gathered up giddy broom, rippling cape, and wild hat. "I've had it with you guys. I've had it with all my powers!" I jammed them into a cardboard box and sealed it with packing tape.

I found a piece of posterboard and made a sign.

Slightly used powers for sale. Cheap.
Cape, broom, and hat—available now.
Make me an offer. I won't refuse.
No money down. Credit to all.

And I set myself up for business on our front steps.

My first customer was a five-year-old boy. He pointed at the sign. "What's that?"

"It says powers for sale. Do you want some?"

"Yes. What are powers?"

"They let you fly, do things like that."

"Do they cost a lot of money?"

"Cheap," I said. "Whatever you want to pay for them."

"I don't know."

"A penny? Do you have a penny?"

He fished in his pocket. "Nope."

I looked in mine. "Me, neither. I'll give them to you for free."

"I don't have a free."

"Well, you can have them anyway."

"Look, there's a grasshopper." And my first customer wandered off.

An hour passed.

My mother came outside and read my sign.

She shook her head and went back in the house.

I counted six bikes, twenty-one cars, two airplanes, and four skateboards. Also a stroller, a baby carriage, and a couple of roller skaters. A few people waved at me, but no one stopped.

Then Mandy and Jennifer strolled past. They stopped and looked at the sign. "Used powers for sale. Cheap," Mandy read. "If they're your powers, Bumble Bee, of course they're cheap."

Maybe I should make Mandy disappear. That would show her! But what if I made Jennifer disappear instead?

Jennifer picked up the hat. "This is kind of cute." She put it on. "Look at me, Mandy."

"Yuck! *Her* hat?" Mandy said. "It probably has lice."

"No lice," I said. "Just snakes." Oh dear! Skinny

green snakes dropped out of the hat and slithered down Jennifer's shoulders and arms.

"Get these off me, Phoebe!" she shrieked, brushing herself frantically. "What kind of trick is this? You did this on purpose, didn't you?"

I snatched the hat from her head and threw it to the ground. "No snakes!" I cried. "No tricks! Snakes go! No snakes!"

The snakes disappeared.

Jennifer staggered away. "I want to go home!"

Mandy kicked the hat and stomped on it. The hat rolled over as if it had been shot.

"That's no way to treat a valuable witch's hat!" I cried.

"Witch's hat? Oh yeah?" Mandy jumped on it again. "That's what I think of you and your so-called witch's hat." She grabbed Jennifer's hand, and they ran down the driveway.

I threw the sign in the garbage can, picked up the cape, broom, and squashed hat, and ran back into the house.

In my room, I shoved everything into a dark corner of my closet and slammed the door. "And stay there!" I yelled.

AN IDEA

In the supermarket, doing an errand for my mother, I met—well, bumped into—Peter Cook in the candy aisle. "Hi, Phoebe," he said, staggering sideways.

"Hi, Peter." I backed away and a box of chocolate bars fell to the floor.

We both bent over to pick them up—and knocked our heads together.

"Sorry," I said.

"Me, too," Peter said.

On hands and knees, we stared at each other.

"What are you doing here?" he asked.

"Buying marshmallows for my mom. She loves them."

"Me, too," he said again. "I mean, my mom, too."

"Wow." I scanned him quickly from head to toe. Everything still seemed to be in place. And the squeak was gone.

"Remember the other day when we walked home from school together?" I said.

Peter blinked. "Sure."

"I made you disappear."

"Yeah!" he said. "It was great!"

"Not for me!" I stood up and tossed a few chocolate bars back on the shelf. "It was a nightmare!"

Peter got to his feet and brushed himself off. "It was the best, most exciting thing that ever happened to me," he said.

"I almost didn't get you back," I reminded him.

"But you did." Peter grabbed my hand. "I knew you'd come through."

I smiled at him.

"Do you still want to come over and have supper in my tree house?" he asked.

I did. I really did! But I was afraid of what I might say or do or destroy. "I can't . . ."

His face fell. "Is it because you're a witch and I'm not?"

"Sort of." Would Peter understand if I said that my powers were like a Midas touch—except that whatever *I* touched got wrecked?

"Maybe another time?" I said.

"Oh, sure. Yeah. I guess so."

We both grabbed our packages of marshmallows and fled in opposite directions down the aisle.

*　　*　　*

When I got home, I went to my room and flung myself on the bed. Now, on top of everything else, I had hurt Peter's feelings. My powers had become like a prison, binding one disaster after another to me. I thought of my poor exasperated mother. Peter in danger of disappearing permanently. Jennifer embarrassed and angry. And Mandy laughing at me.

My face got hot remembering how Mandy stomped on my hat. What good were my powers, anyway? Every time I saw her, she did something mean to me. And got away with it. Why didn't I step on *her* feet or stomp *her* hat or shove *her* back?

From inside the closet came a loud tapping. My broom wanting out. Or was it telling me something?

The broom banged louder on the wall, as if to say, "Yeah! Stomp on Mandy!"

"Yes, I'd like to. But be quiet now. I'm thinking!"

I closed my eyes and tried to concentrate, but instead I fell asleep and dreamed that I saw Jacky.

She said, *"You have to learn to control your powers, dearie."*

"I know! I need lessons, Jacky. Not from a piece of paper. From you!"

"Sorry, dearie. We told you. No lessons now."

Her gray hair was pulled back by combs with cats etched on them, and she was carrying a battered orange knapsack on her back. The light caught the combs in her hair, and the cats winked at me.

"Just a short lesson? A little one? A mini lesson?" I pleaded.

"Sorry, dearie. No time, no time, no time . . ."

"What am I supposed to do, Jackie? Can't you help me? I'm afraid to even play with my friends now! What kind of a life is that?"

The cats winked again. *"You know the answer!"*

"No, I don't!"

I woke up furious. How was *I* supposed to know what to do. That was the witches' job, not mine. I jumped off the bed and kicked the closet door, hard. The broom banged back.

"Nyah!" I yelled.

Suddenly I *did* have an idea. It was a small,

modest idea, not the kind Andelica or Mesmerelda would have thought up, but still, it was something.

It might work, I told myself.

At least I could try it.

I opened the closet door, grabbed the broom, and wedged it under my arm. I put on my cape and plopped my witch's hat on my head.

"We're going to the cemetery," I said.

The broom squirmed excitedly.

"We've got work to do. Like my mother said, 'You have to walk before you can fly.'"

I had never learned to walk as a witch. I had gotten too many powers too fast, and I'd never learned the basics. What I needed was to begin at the beginning.

And if the witches wouldn't help me, I'd help myself. If I could.

If they didn't have the time to give me lessons, I'd give them to myself. I'd try, anyway.

Something had to give. It was either me—or my powers.

THE TAMING
OF THE BROOM

The broom swooped past, daring me to catch it.

"Down. Come down here *at once!*" I commanded.

It ignored me.

It flew over my head, teasing me. I grabbed it as it passed. It wiggled and bounced like a little kid about to go to the fair.

"No, we're not going to fly," I said. "Calm down!"

It kept leaping into the air.

"This is witch school," I announced. "First we're going to learn to sweep. You have to sweep before you can fly, you know."

We were in the cemetery, right near the tree I'd fallen out of into the witches' circle. There was no one around, except for me and the broom. Leaves covered the ground.

I pointed the broom toward them. "Sweep," I said.

The broom just hung there.

"Sweep the leaves in a pile! Pile. P-i-l-e. Leaves. L-e-a-v-e-s. Get it?"

No response.

"Are you really that dumb? Or are you just playing hard to get?"

The broom flew from my hand and languidly swept over the leaves, which fluttered and rose into the air.

"Good!" I said. "That's the way!"

The praise went to the broom's head. It swept faster—and faster. The leaves whirled and spun, spun and whirled, until they were a miniature hurricane.

"Stop!" I yelled.

The broom halted in midair and flipped its straw at me.

Training it was going to be even more of a challenge than I had thought.

I grabbed it again with both hands. "I see that we'll just have to do this together."

The broom had other ideas. It jerked me off my feet and into the air.

Then it tried to get rid of me.

It bucked and spun like a horse trying to throw its rider. But I wouldn't let go.

It headed for the pond, turned me upside down, and shook me until I dropped headfirst into the water.

I swam to shore and came out dripping wet and fighting mad. The broom hovered over me in a smug way.

Its attitude annoyed me. "It's one thing to be difficult," I said, "it's another to gloat about it!"

I filled my witch's hat with water and dumped it over the broom. "Take that, if you're so smart!" I said. "And that!"

The broom squirmed and twisted in protest.

"I know, I know. I'd rather be somewhere else, too," I said. "But remember? 'You have to walk before you can fly.' In this case, sweep. We're here to practice sweeping. Get it now?"

This time we swept together. We swept leaves. Then we swept more leaves. We swept until there was a pile of leaves under the tree as tall as me.

"Now, you know how to do it." I said. "So let me see you do it by yourself."

I pointed. "Sweep those twigs into a pile."

The broom leaped out of my hand, rushed over to the twigs, and swept them up into a heap.

I felt a proud glow, like a mother who had just

taught her baby to speak. The broom had finally learned something. And I was the one who had taught it. My first real success as a witch. Wait until I told Mesmerelda, Jacky, and Andelica!

All this training had worked up my appetite and worn me out. That broom was one tough customer. "Go take a break," I said to it. I flung off my cape and hat, sat in the sun, and thought about eating a nice juicy red apple. I was hungry. Maybe I could conjure one up. Of course, I'd have to have a spell.

"Candy apple, red and sweet; you are what I want to eat. Apple bright, apple near; come on, apple, *appear!*"

I looked hopefully up into the tree. But no apple fell into my hand.

Instead, Mandy stood before me.

MANDY APPLE

Mandy was dressed in red. Her eyes were small and unfriendly, like two shiny apple seeds.

Just the sight of her made me feel weak all over. "Hello," I whispered.

"What am I doing here?" she demanded. "And where's Jennifer? We were just walking together!"

"I brought you," I admitted. "Only I wanted a different kind of apple!"

Mandy was staring at the old gravestones. "You hang out in a *cemetery?* You're weirder than I thought." She smiled and looked really mean. "Got you alone now, Bumbling Bee. Exactly what I've been waiting for!"

I looked around, wishing that my spell had brought

Jennifer as well as Mandy. "Hello? Hello!" I called, just in case. "Anybody here? Jennifer? Jennifer!"

Mandy leaped toward me.

I jumped aside, tripped, and fell face first in the mud.

"Ha-ha!" Mandy shook an overhanging tree branch, and crab apples rained down on my head like stones.

I picked up a crab apple and threw it.

"You couldn't hit me if I stood right next to you, Dumble Bee!"

She was right. The apple skidded past her.

I staggered to my feet. I needed my magic right now, if I ever did. Only my cape, broom, and hat were nowhere in sight.

I groped for my bead, but I'd forgotten to bring it.

I tried to say a spell, but my tongue was dry.

Mandy's fists were clenched and her legs were running full speed toward me.

My legs felt like spaghetti.

I scanned the trees for a clear path out of the cemetery and wondered if I could outrun her. She was quick and wiry, while I was slow and round.

I stumbled away. Mandy was right behind me.

"Truce!" I cried.

"Chicken!" She caught me, yanked me by the collar, and reeled me in. Her eyes gleamed. "I'm going to finish you off, once and for all."

And then Jennifer walked into the clearing. "Mandy! There you are!" She paused. "Bee? What are you doing here? What are you two doing together?"

"Nothing," Mandy shrugged. "Just a little argument."

"She's trying to beat me up!" I yelled.

"We're having a fight," Mandy corrected me. "Little me against the big bad witch. I don't even have a chance! But now that you're here, Jennifer, we can even the balance. Two ordinary girls against a witch. That's a fair fight, isn't it?"

Jennifer stared at Mandy; she stared at me; she stared at the ground.

"Let's get her, Jennifer!" Mandy said.

"You wouldn't hurt an old friend, would you, Jennifer?" I said.

Jennifer took a step toward Mandy, then a step toward me, then stopped.

"What's the matter?" Mandy said. "You're not scared, are you?"

Jennifer frowned. "I don't like fights."

"I already told you, Jennifer, this is different. Two of us against this witch." Mandy yanked my arm for emphasis. "If you don't help me, who knows what could happen?"

"Yeah, I might get away in one piece," I muttered.

Jennifer kicked at some twigs. "This is stupid. Why don't you just forget it, Mandy? Let's go back to our walk."

"That's the spirit," I agreed. "Forget about it."

Mandy's eyes snapped. Her cheeks blazed red. "Jennifer, are you on my side or not?"

"Yes . . . ," Jennifer said.

"If you're on my side, you fight when I ask you to."

Jennifer didn't say anything.

"Well?" Mandy demanded. "Are you or aren't you?"

Suddenly Mandy shoved me as hard as she could.

"Ooommph!" I went down on my back.

Jennifer gasped. "Phoebe!"

"Phoebe . . . ," Mandy mimicked.

Jennifer stamped her foot. "Why are you always so mean?"

"*What?*" She gave Jennifer a shove.

"You're such a bully!" Jennifer yelled.

"Take that back or else!"

"I won't. I'm sick of you!"

My head jerked up. "Jennifer," I said. "Is that really you? Can I believe my ears?"

Mandy couldn't believe her ears, either. "You're calling me a bully? No one calls Mandy names." She grabbed Jennifer and shook her hard.

"Ow! Stop! Don't!" Jennifer cried. "Let me go."

Suddenly I was really angry. Mandy was hurting my best friend. Well, anyway, the person who'd been my best friend for more years than anyone else.

With a roar like a hundred witches, I leaped up and hauled Mandy off Jennifer. "Leave Jennifer alone!" I yelled. "And me, too!"

Mandy made a gurgling noise that sounded like water going down the drain. "Wh . . . wha . . . wha . . ."

She was so surprised, she couldn't even get out a word.

I was surprised, too. Was that really me? Had I just yanked Mandy off Jennifer? Defended both Jennifer and myself?

"Come on, Jennifer," I said. "Let's go."

"What about me?" Mandy asked.

"What about you?" Jennifer said, linking arms with me. "Go home!"

"Yeah. Get lost. We don't want you around," I added.

Mandy stared at me as if she'd never seen me before.

Perhaps she hadn't.

COVEN GIRL

"Do you think our mud pie is done, Bee?"

I looked in the oven. "Smells great, Mom! Maybe ten more minutes."

Suddenly the curtains billowed wildly. A cat in the yard yowled. There was a clap of thunder, followed by a blinding flash of lightning. I blinked my eyes and there were Andelica, Mesmerelda, and Jacky standing in the middle of our kitchen.

My mother and I stared at them. Jacky and Mesmerelda were wearing sleek gray rain suits with red rubber boots; the beautiful witch was resplendent in a dark green rain cape and boots and a jumpsuit the color of grass.

"The witches of the Fifth Sector have sent us to

119

you," announced Andelica. "We are authorized to present you their official views."

"Do come in." My mother hastily wiped her hands on a towel and ushered the witches into the living room.

"To what do we owe this honor?" she asked.

"We've come to let you know we'll be giving Phoebe lessons from now on," said Jacky.

"We'll see if she can learn anything," Mesmerelda grumbled.

"Of course she can!" said Jacky, poking Mesmerelda with her elbow.

"What kind of lessons?" my mother asked. "She's already tried the guitar, roller-skating, and pottery."

"Witch lessons, naturally," said Andelica. Her necklace was green, too, and it hummed like a cricket.

My mother laughed, but nobody else did.

"I'm finally going to get lessons," I said. "Great!" Maybe I could even risk having supper in Peter's tree house soon.

My mother looked from one witch to another. Then she looked at me.

"Witch lessons?" my mother said, at last. "My Phoebe is a witch?"

"An apprentice witch," corrected Andelica.

"Accidental apprentice witch," I added.

My mother sat down suddenly on the couch.

"No one can believe it at first." Jacky rose to the ceiling and floated over our heads. "It took my own mother two years to believe it."

I ran to get my broom. "Watch this, Mom."

I hopped on. "Okay. Gracefully," I whispered to the broom. "Let's do it like Jacky did!" We grazed the top of the couch, and wobbled across the room, sweeping only a few dozen magazines off the coffee table.

My mother rushed over and hugged me. "Phoebe, my little coven girl. I always knew you were special. This calls for a celebration!"

We all had slices of chocolate mud pie and cups of apple juice.

When the witches left, they gave me a gift—a piece of blue woven cloth folded into a square no bigger than a thumbnail. I gasped when I opened it. It was one of the witches' story tapestries. Embroidered in bright threads was the story of my day in the cemetery. Me, sweeping leaves with the broom. Then leaping on Mandy. Then walking home arm in arm with Jennifer.

I felt a glow of pride and strength. It had been quite a day. Broom training and Mandy taming. Jennifer and I were friends again. And best of all, I hadn't needed any powers to defeat Mandy; I had done it on my own. I folded the story tapestry carefully and put it in my pocket.

24
ANOTHER ONE

Andelica's eyes were closed as she paced and chanted. The beads on her necklace blazed as if they were speaking their own language.

I leaned on my broom, quiet, waiting, as she paced her circle faster and faster. Would I ever be a witch like her? I looked up into the tree that had started it all, the tree I'd fallen out of all those weeks ago.

Andelica's words, which had started as a slow murmur, built gradually to a deep rumbling chant.

Clouds darkened the sky, and a cold wind whirled through the grass.

Andelica chanted. "Stars, bars, witches and riches . . ."

She moved faster, almost spinning. "Yellow toads and sticky roads . . . Send them all to me!" The words clanged and crashed like metal pots.

Then came the other witches, a long streaking mass.

Capes whipped out. Branches shook and leaves rained to the ground. "All here," Jacky cried.

Suddenly something plummeted from the tree and landed in the middle of our circle.

Peter Cook stood up. "Oops," he said.

"Peter!" I said. "What are you doing here?"

He brushed off his sweatshirt. It was covered with leaves and twigs. "Hi, Phoebe."

"You fell into our circle," I said. "That makes you a—"

"A boy?" Mesmerelda hissed. "We haven't had one of those in two hundred and eighty-seven years!"

"Two hundred and eighty-eight," Jacky corrected.

"Get rid of him," Mesmerelda said. "Right now. Fast!"

Peter's face fell. He looked at me. I hopped on my broom and hovered over him. "Don't worry," I whispered. "It'll be all right."

Andelica took out a little book and wet her thumb. She flipped through the pages. "Another one," she sighed. "But it says right here, 'The accidental witch . . .'"